Favourite
Princess
Tales

Favourite
Princess
Tales

Published by Alligator Books Limited
Gadd House, Arcadia Avenue
London N3 2JU

Printed in China   12245

Beauty
and the
Beast

Once upon a time there was a very wealthy sea merchant who owned a magnificent house and lived there with his three daughters. The merchant was so rich, he made sure that his three girls had everything they wished for, whatever the cost.

Unfortunately his two elder daughters became lazy and spoilt. Day after day they demanded more and more expensive gifts, and if they didn't get what they wanted, they sulked until they did!

His younger daughter was quite different. She asked for nothing at all except the love of her dear father. He had fondly named her Beauty when she was small, she meant so much to him. This made the elder sisters jealous. They teased Beauty about her name, laughing at her because she enjoyed music and books and tending to her father's lovely gardens.

They were only interested in parties and dancing and cared for no one except themselves. "Why stay at home every night wasting your time on boring books and dull music when you could be out having fun?" they taunted.

In the evening when Beauty was at home with her father, he would tell her about his fleet of trading ships that sailed the oceans, and how the rich cargoes they brought back had made him so wealthy.

Beauty loved to hear her father talk and tell stories. She was so proud of him, for he was a very clever and successful man.

One morning a messenger arrived bringing dreadful news. Every one of the merchant's great ships had been wrecked during fierce storms, and their valuable cargoes had sunk to the bottom of the sea. Overnight the merchant had lost his fortune.

"We must move from this grand house," sighed the merchant. "My money is gone and all I have left is a small farm in the country."

"Then we are lucky indeed!" cried Beauty cheerfully. "With a little land we can grow our own vegetables, we'll keep chickens and maybe a cow."

"We shall move there right away," said the merchant smiling at Beauty. "No one will starve and we shall have a roof over our heads. We are lucky indeed, my dear!"

And so it was that the merchant and his family lived together in the tiny farmhouse for a whole year.

The two elder daughters hated the country and they complained each time they were asked to do the smallest task.

Beauty, on the other hand, enjoyed her new life. She learned how to cook. She grew all sorts of vegetables and cared for all the animals.

Then one day the merchant received some marvellous news. One of his ships was not lost at sea after all but had sailed safely into a port nearby.

The merchant was overjoyed. "I must go and claim it immediately," he told his three daughters. "When I sell the cargo we shall be rich once more!"

The merchant promised to bring back lots of expensive presents. This made his two elder daughters dance up and down with excitement.

"I don't need a gift," said Beauty as she kissed her father goodbye. "Pick a lovely pink rose and give it to me on your safe return."

When the merchant reached the port his joy quickly turned to despair. Thieves had stolen the valuable cargo and then set fire to his ship.

When the merchant headed back home that night it grew so dark and stormy, he took a wrong turn in the road, and lost his way.

Strange howling noises came from the woods nearby, shadowy shapes darted around him and pairs of glowing eyes peered out from the gloom. The terrified merchant ran for his life!

11

All of a sudden, the rain stopped, the storm passed and all was peace and quiet. The merchant could only gaze in astonishment... in front of him stood the most magnificent castle with lights shining from every window.

How relieved Beauty's father was. Perhaps here he could find a night's shelter, for above the open door of the castle was written... 'Enter weary traveller and welcome!'

Once inside, the merchant searched through many splendid rooms, but found no one. The castle seemed empty.

In one of the rooms a fire was burning brightly, and a table was set with a feast fit for a king. The hungry merchant helped himself to the delicious food. In the corner was a comfortable bed, so he lay down and fell fast asleep.

On waking next morning, the merchant was amazed to discover a fine suit of clothes to replace his own.

Breakfast had been laid on the table. When he had eaten, the merchant went outside and found a bush covered with pink roses growing by the wall. He remembered his promise to Beauty but as he reached to pick a bloom there was a tremendous roar. To the merchant's horror, a ferocious-looking creature came bounding towards him.

"How dare you steal my roses?" growled the Beast
and he snarled at the trembling merchant, "I have
given you food, and shelter. You have repayed me by
stealing my precious roses. Now you must die!"

The merchant begged for forgiveness. "Please don't
kill me, sire. The rose I picked is for the youngest of my
three daughters."

The Beast listened carefully, and when he heard
about Beauty, he made a very strange bargain with
the merchant.

"I will spare your life. However, you must promise
that after a month you will bring back one of your
daughters to stay with me. She must come willingly,
or you must return to die!"

Hastily the merchant gave his word, although he had no intention of keeping it.

"Go now!" the Beast commanded. "Take this gift of gold and jewels to your family."

The merchant felt suddenly tired and closed his eyes. When he opened them, he was back home.

As soon as the two elder daughters saw all the treasure they were delighted. But their joy turned to sorrow as their father gave Beauty her rose and told his awful tale.

The minute Beauty heard of her father's solemn promise, she knew it had to be kept.

"You are not going to die!" she told him. "Take me back to stay with the Beast for I cannot let you break your vow."

So one month later Beauty and her father set off. Strangely the journey seemed to take no time at all.

"What a perfectly lovely place," Beauty gasped as the castle came into view.

Quaking with fright, the merchant led Beauty inside. Just as before the castle seemed deserted. There were no servants, although a table had been set for two in the grand hall.

All of a sudden a door opened and in strode the Beast. "You are welcome here, Beauty," he said in a gruff but kind voice. "Did you come of your own free will?"

"I did, sire," whispered Beauty.

The Beast turned to the merchant and said sternly, "Now you must go home!" and he left the room.

But when he had gone, the poor girl began to cry as she wandered through the castle alone and frightened.

Before long she came to a door with the words, BEAUTY'S ROOM, written on it.

Imagine her surprise when she stepped inside... it was a room fit for a princess! On the table by the bed the Beast had placed a magic mirror. As she turned it round Beauty read,

There is no need for you to fear,
Dear Beauty, you are welcome here.
Use this mirror as you may,
Your every wish it will obey.

This made Beauty feel better. Beauty soon lost her fear of the Beast and began to enjoy her new life. She read books and played music, and in the afternoon she walked with the Beast in the magnificent castle gardens. Every day the Beast asked Beauty the same question. "Beauty, will you marry me?"

Although she had grown very fond of the Beast, Beauty would always shake her head in reply.

One morning as Beauty happened to look into the magic mirror, she glimpsed her father looking very sick. Straight away she begged the Beast to allow her to go home.

The Beast heaved a great sigh. "You may go, but I fear you will never return and I shall die of grief," said the Beast sadly as he handed Beauty a magic ring. "If, of your own free will, you decide to return to me, you only have to blow on this ring."

Beauty felt suddenly tired and closed her eyes. When she opened them, she found herself back home with her father.

The merchant was overjoyed to see his dear daughter and felt better at once. The two were so happy to be together again, the weeks that followed just flew by.

Then one night Beauty dreamed she was walking in the castle gardens, and there, lying quite still on the ground, was the Beast.

"My poor Beast is dead because I have not returned!" cried Beauty the next morning. Quickly she reached for the magic ring, closed her eyes and blew on it gently.

In less than a moment she was back in the castle gardens kneeling beside the Beast.

"I promise I will never leave you again," sobbed Beauty. "Dear Beast, please don't die."

When the Beast heard Beauty's kind words, he opened his eyes and whispered, "Beauty, will you marry me?"

Straight away Beauty answered, "Yes, dear Beast, I will marry you."

As she said this a great crash was heard. Music filled the air, and hundreds of glittering lights shone... in that instant the Beast changed into a handsome Prince.

Beauty was too startled to speak as the Prince stood before her.

"Dear Beauty, you have set me free at last," he said smiling at her. "Long ago, a wicked enchantress turned me into a hideous Beast. Only the true love of a beautiful woman could break her evil spell. When you agreed to marry me, I became a Prince once more."

Very soon a splendid wedding was held at the castle. Beauty and her handsome Prince were married and lived happily every after.

The kind-hearted Prince asked Beauty's father to live with them at the castle, and the merchant stayed there for the rest of his days.

He took care of the roses in the garden, especially the pink ones.

And he made quite sure the castle door was always open to welcome weary travellers!

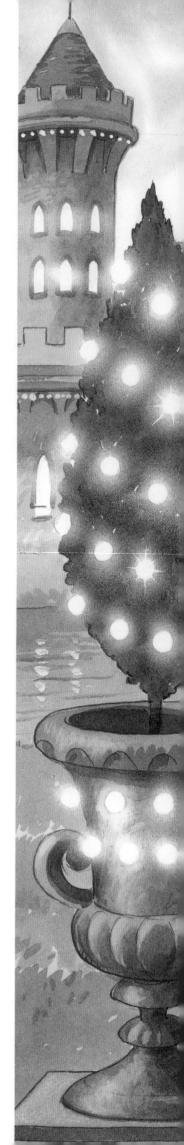

Cinderella

Once upon a time there lived a rich baron. He had a loving family and a fine house with beautiful gardens. He was a very happy man indeed.

One terrible day, his wife fell ill and, soon after, passed away. But he wasn't left all alone. For he had a beautiful young daughter, and now he had been left to bring her up on his own.

After some years the baron married again. He soon discovered that his second wife was cruel and selfish.

She had two daughters of her own who were like her in every way. They complained, they whined, they moaned and groaned, they even stamped their feet in temper. Unfortunately all their sulking and pouting had turned them into a very unattractive pair!

How different they were from the baron's own lovely child, who was gentle and kind to everyone.

One sad day the baron became very ill and died, now his poor daughter had nobody to take care of her except her cruel stepmother and her horrid daughters.

As time went on the baron's daughter became more and more beautiful. Her stepsisters were so jealous of her good looks they began to treat her like a servant, and her cruel stepmother gave her the hardest and dirtiest tasks in the house.

They ordered the poor girl to scrub all the floors, wash every pot and polish every pan. Then there were carpets to brush, windows to wash and stairs to polish every single day.

Her two lazy stepsisters did no work whatsoever, they just sat around giving orders and complaining.

Every night when her work was done, the weary girl would go into the kitchen and sit by the fire amongst the cinders.

When the two mean stepsisters saw her grubby hands and feet, they called her "Cinderella."

One morning a letter arrived from the palace inviting everyone to a Grand Ball.

"It's from the Prince himself," the stepmother said grinning at her daughters, "no doubt the Prince will choose one of you to be his bride."

"Give it to me!" screamed one of the girls as she tried to snatch the invitation.

"It's mine, mine, mine!" shrieked the other, stamping her feet.

"May I go too?" asked Cinderella timidly.

"Certainly not!" yelled all three.

"I believe the invitation is for me too," said Cinderella quietly.

This made the stepsisters hoot with laughter. "Do you really think the Prince would even glance at you in your ragged clothes?" taunted one of them.

Then the other joined in. "Cinderella looked stunning at the Grand Ball tonight... she was wearing a ripped skirt and a grubby apron."

How cruel, how unkind. Cinderella hung her head to hide her tears.

"Get on with your chores at once!"snapped her stepmother, "and when you have finished, help my daughters get ready for the ball tonight."

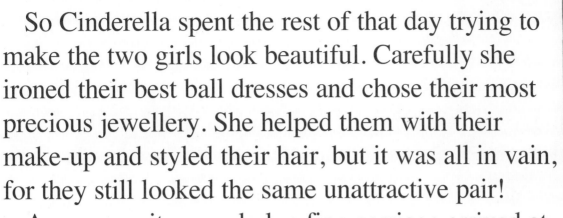

So Cinderella spent the rest of that day trying to make the two girls look beautiful. Carefully she ironed their best ball dresses and chose their most precious jewellery. She helped them with their make-up and styled their hair, but it was all in vain, for they still looked the same unattractive pair!

As soon as it grew dark a fine carriage arrived at the front door, and the stepmother and her daughters drove off to the ball.

Feeling very disappointed, Cinderella went back into the kitchen and sat by the fire.

As she gazed at the flickering flames she imagined herself at the ball, and maybe, just maybe, dancing with the Prince himself.

Suddenly Cinderella thought she heard music. "It must be coming from the palace," she sighed. "Oh how I wish I could go to the ball!"

"So you shall, my dear!" said a kindly voice, and there, hovering beside her, was a fairy wearing a hat covered in tiny bells.

"Who are you?" Cinderella gasped.

"Your Fairy Godmother, my dear, and I'm here to grant your wish!" And the bells on her hat jingled softly as she moved.

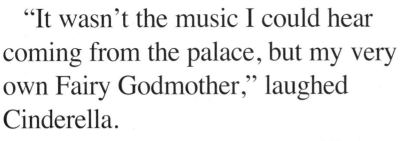

"It wasn't the music I could hear coming from the palace, but my very own Fairy Godmother," laughed Cinderella.

"Now let's get busy, or you'll never get to the ball!" said the fairy, then she asked Cinderella to bring her the biggest pumpkin she could find, and any rats and mice that had been caught in the trap.

When Cinderella had done that, her Fairy Godmother waved her magic wand, and as the sparkling fairy dust fluttered all around, something magical happened...

...the pumpkin turned into a magnificent golden coach, the four mice became four silver-grey horses, one of the rats changed into a smart coachman, the other a handsome footman.

When the Fairy Godmother glanced at Cinderella she gave a little shriek, "Oh my goodness! You can't go to a ball dressed like that!"

And with a wave of her magic wand, she transformed Cinderella's ragged clothes into a beautiful ball gown, and on her feet were a pair of glittering glass slippers.

"Now you are ready to go to the ball," said the Fairy Godmother, "but listen carefully, you must leave the palace before the clock strikes twelve, for then my magic ends. Everything will go back as it was, and you will be dressed in rags once again."

33

Although Cinderella had never been so excited in her whole life, she didn't forget to thank the Fairy Godmother for making her wish come true.

Then the footman helped her into her wonderful golden coach, the coachman cracked his whip, and they set off for the palace.

"Make haste, my dear, or you'll be late!" called her Fairy Godmother as she waved goodbye. "And remember to be back before midnight!"

All the guests had arrived and were dancing when Cinderella entered the ballroom. The musicians stopped playing and everyone turned to gaze.

Who was this beautiful stranger? Was she a royal princess from a distant kingdom?

Every single guest at the ball that night wondered who this lovely girl could be, especially Cinderella's stepmother and her daughters, who didn't recognise her at all.

When the Prince stepped forward to greet Cinderella, he took one look and fell in love with her.

34

That evening at the ball the Prince would dance with no-one except Cinderella. He was so enchanted by her beauty he never let her out of his sight for a moment, and they danced together all night long.

Cinderella was so graceful and behaved with such charm, the other guests couldn't fail to admire her.

Even her stepmother was impressed. "Who can this attractive girl be? She has captured the Prince's heart, and that's for sure!"

Cinderella was so happy dancing with the Prince she forgot about the time, and as the palace clock began to strike twelve she remembered her Fairy Godmother's warning.

Before the Prince could stop her, Cinderella rushed out of the ballroom door. Halfway down the staircase she lost one of her glittering glass slippers - but there was no time to stop and pick it up. Cinderella could hear the Prince calling her. She had to get out of sight before she changed back into her rags.

Then on the very last strike of midnight, as Cinderella reached the bottom of the staircase... the golden coach turned back into a pumpkin, the mice and rats became themselves again, and instead of her beautiful ball gown, the poor girl was dressed in her ragged clothes once more.

Quickly, before anyone noticed her, Cinderella hurried through the palace gates and ran back home in the dark. And to her surprise, when she put her hand into her apron pocket, there was the other glittering glass slipper.

The Prince and his servants searched the palace grounds until dawn, but it was all in vain, his beautiful dancing partner had vanished and the Prince was brokenhearted.

Then, as he climbed wearily up the stairs to the palace, the Prince found the glass slipper that Cinderella had left behind.

"Let it be known throughout the kingdom," the Prince declared, "I will marry only the girl who can wear this slipper!"

Early next morning the search began. The Prince and his servant visited house after house with the glass slipper. Every girl tried it on, but it fitted none of them.

Cinderella's stepsisters were so eager to become the Prince's bride, that when it came to their turn, they began to fight over the slipper.

"It's mine!" yelled one trying hard to squeeze her clumsy foot inside.

"It belongs to me!" screamed the other as she snatched the slipper from her sister.

However it was no use at all... their feet were far too big.

"Let me try on the slipper," said Cinderella who had been standing in the shadows.

"What? You marry the Prince?" shrieked her stepmother. "Don't be ridiculous!"

The very moment the Prince saw Cinderella, he was sure he had found the girl of his dreams. Both of them just knew that the slipper would fit perfectly and, of course, it did.

The stepmother and her daughters were speechless. They realised that the lovely girl at the ball was really Cinderella. They were still lost for words when Cinderella pulled the matching glass slipper from her apron pocket and put it on.

The Prince asked Cinderella to be his bride, and she gladly agreed.

Suddenly, Cinderella's Fairy Godmother appeared. "If you're going to marry the Prince you will need a splendid dress," she said waving her magic wand, and as the sparkling fairy dust fluttered around something magical happened.

Cinderella's ragged clothes became the most dazzling dress and the very next day she and the Prince were married. The whole kingdom joined in the celebrations, and everyone lived happily ever after...

...as for Cinderella's stepmother and her stepsisters, all three were part of the happy ending.

As they were truly sorry for their mean and selfish ways, Cinderella forgave them and invited them to live at the palace.

And before too long, they became as loving and kind as the people around them. Perhaps the Fairy Godmother's magic dust helped!

Sleeping Beauty

Once upon a time there lived a King and Queen. For years they had longed for a child, then to their delight, the Queen gave birth to a baby girl. Great was the rejoicing at the royal palace and throughout the whole kingdom.

As the King and Queen gazed fondly at their beautiful little daughter they felt their happiness was complete.

"We must celebrate our baby's arrival with a great banquet here at the palace!" said the King.

"And we must make quite sure to invite all the good fairies in the land," added the Queen, for she hoped that each one would give the baby a gift that would help her in life.

As soon as the arrangements had been made for the banquet, invitations were sent out from the palace, and six good fairies who lived in distant parts of the kingdom were asked to be godmothers to the baby Princess.

The King ordered that a special place was to be set at the table, with a golden plate and a silver goblet for each of the good fairies.

But unfortunately... and no one really knows how it happened... when the invitations were sent out, a mistake was made!

On the day of the banquet guests travelled from near and far for the happy occasion.

When the time came for the six good fairies to give the little Princess their gifts, they gathered round her cradle.

"I give her the gift of happiness," said the first fairy.

"My gift is wisdom," said the second.

"She will always be thoughtful and kind," said the third.

"And loving and giving," promised the fourth.

Then as the fifth fairy bestowed her gift of charm and gracefulness on the Princess, the room suddenly grew dark as a shadow fell across the baby's cradle.

The King and Queen shuddered, for standing close by was a wicked-looking fairy shaking with rage, looking at them angrily.

Straight away the sixth fairy realised that something was wrong, so before anyone noticed, she hid herself.

"Where was my invitation?" screamed the furious fairy. "Where is my golden plate and silver goblet? You will pay for this!"

When the King realised that the fairy had been overlooked, he said he was truly sorry and begged her to sit next to him at the table. The King wanted her to feel special.

This only made the fairy angrier for she took it as an insult.

Then, to everyone's horror, she pointed a bony finger at the baby Princess and shouted, "When you are sixteen, you will prick your finger on a spindle and die!"

Everyone in the room fell silent. Not one of the guests could believe the wicked fairy's terrible curse.

Just at that moment, the sixth fairy came out of her hiding place.

"Your Majesties," she said to the King and Queen. "My gift to the Princess is not yet given. Although I do not have the power to stop the wicked fairy's spell, I do have the power to change it."

Oh, how the King and Queen and all their guests wished this could be true.

"The Princess will not die," promised the fairy. "She will fall into a deep sleep for a hundred years. One day a Prince will wake her with a kiss and the spell will be broken!"

No words can describe the King and Queen's joy when they heard what the fairy said. "How can we ever thank you?" sobbed the Queen drying her tears. "Promise that you will send for me if ever I am needed," replied the fairy.

Before the six good fairies returned to distant parts of the kingdom, they decided to cast a powerful spell.

"Together we summon all our magic powers and banish you from this land!"

The wicked fairy stared in disbelief as a terrifying whirlwind twirled her high into the air and she was gone forever.

Needless to say, that very same day, the King issued an order to protect the Princess from harm.

Never again were any of his subjects allowed to spin to make thread, and every spindle and spinning wheel throughout the kingdom was destroyed at once.

Messengers were sent throughout the land to make sure that everyone knew of the King's strict new law.

Before too long there were no spinning wheels left, and after a while people forgot how to spin altogether.

Time passed and the Princess grew up into a beautiful young girl. She was graceful and charming, loving and giving. In fact, she possessed all the gifts that the good fairies had given her as a baby.

That seemed so long ago, the wicked fairy's curse was all but forgotten...

...until one day. The Princess was sixteen years old and she was wandering through the palace with her little dog by her side.

"I do believe you want to go exploring," laughed the Princess as the little dog raced down a passage and pushed open a creaking old door. A winding staircase led to a tiny room at the very top of the palace.

"We've never been up here before," said the Princess as she picked up her little dog. "I don't want you to get lost, you little mischief!"

Then the Princess heard a voice.

"I have a visitor at last. Come in my dear!" In the corner of the tiny room sat a dear old lady spinning cotton.

"What are you doing?" the Princess asked, for as you know she had never seen anything like it before.

Now by a strange chance, the dear old lady had never been told of the law banning spindles and spinning wheels, nor did she know that her young visitor was the Princess.

"Why, I'm spinning, my dear," said the old lady. "Would you like to try?"

Eagerly the Princess put down her little dog and reached for the spindle. She was eager to learn how to spin.

The very moment she touched it, the sharp point of the spindle pricked her finger and she fell to the floor in a deep sleep.

The poor old lady was
so dismayed she didn't
know what to do. But
the Princess's little dog
barked so loudly, the palace
servants who were close
by came rushing up the
winding staircase.

They tried to wake the
Princess, but it was in vain,
nothing could rouse her.

When the King and
Queen saw their lovely
daughter they knew that
the spell had come true.

The Princess would sleep for one hundred years, and when she woke everyone in the palace would be dead and gone.

Servants carried her to her most beautiful room in the palace. There she was gently placed on a bed with silken covers and satin pillows.

"We must search for the sixth fairy as we promised so long ago," sobbed the Queen.

"It shall be done," said the King sadly.

Now the sixth fairy was wise as well as good, and when she heard what had happened to the Princess, she knew exactly what to do.

She sped to the palace without delay and began to weave her powerful magic.

Immediately everyone in the palace was bewitched by the fairy's spell and fell into a deep sleep.

The King and Queen with their maids-in-waiting, the guards who were marching, the pages who were bowing, even the cooks who were busy with dinner... all would sleep for a hundred years!

"When the Princess awakes, you will all wake up too," the fairy whispered as she left them to their dreams.

54

Then before she returned to a distant part of the kingdom, the good fairy waved her wand and a thick hedge of thorns sprang up around the palace, so dense that only the very tops of the tallest towers could be seen. And this is how it stayed for one hundred years. No one ever ventured near the palace, they were too afraid!

As time passed it was just the older folk who remembered their parents' tales of the Sleeping Beauty - a lovely Princess who could be awakened only by the kiss of a Prince.

Then one day, a handsome young Prince came riding
by. Suddenly in the distance, he caught a glimpse of the
topmost towers of the palace glistening in the sunlight.

The Prince had never visited that part of the country
before, so he was curious to find out who lived there.

As he stared at the thick thorns in front of him, an
old man gathering sticks came by. The Prince listened
spellbound to the incredible story of the sleeping
Princess, and he was determined to wake her himself!

Imagine his amazement when the thorns parted, and
before him lay a pathway to the palace!

Perhaps you may think this was magic, or maybe the
good fairy was nearby... who knows?

When the Prince reached the palace there was a strange stillness everywhere. He searched the silent rooms and found plenty of servants... but every single one of them was fast asleep!

At last he came to the most magnificent room of all. There on a bed with silken covers and satin pillows, the loveliest girl you can imagine lay sleeping.

The Prince was enchanted, he had found the Sleeping Beauty.

As soon as the Prince saw the sleeping Princess, he fell in love with her, for he had never seen anyone more beautiful in his life.

He bent over to kiss her gently and at once the spell was broken. The Princess opened her eyes and smiled at the handsome young Prince.

"I have waited so long for you," she whispered happily. The palace was no longer bewitched and everyone woke up and carried on with the tasks they began one hundred years ago!

The guards stood to attention, the maids-in-waiting scurried to and fro, the pages bowed politely and the cooks carried on making dinner.

The King and Queen were overjoyed to see their daughter and to meet the Prince. For the hundred years were at an end, and the good fairy's spell had come true at last.

They had a huge party at the palace and invited everyone they knew. Before very long, and to everyone's delight, Sleeping Beauty married her handsome Prince.

And it was in the palace they lived with the King and Queen happily every after.

The good fairy continued to watch over them for the rest of their days.

Snow White

Once upon a time in a land far, far away a beautiful princess was born.

As the King and Queen gazed at their baby daughter, the Queen sighed with happiness and said, "Her skin is so fair, it is pure and white as the snow in winter."

"Then we will call her Snow White," said the King with a smile.

But very soon after little Snow White was born, the Queen died, and the King was left sad and alone.

A few years went by and the King remarried. Although the new Queen was very beautiful, she was wicked and cruel and oh, so vain.

In her room hung a magic mirror. No one was allowed to look into the mirror except the Queen herself.

Now the Queen couldn't bear to think that anyone was lovelier than her, so every day she would stand in front of her mirror and ask,

"Mirror, mirror on the wall,
  Who is the fairest of them all?"

And the mirror would always reply, "You, oh Queen, are the fairest of them all!"
Sometimes, when she was still small, Snow White would take a peep at her stepmother as she looked into her magic mirror.

As time passed Snow White grew more and more beautiful.

61

Then one terrible day, the Queen stood in front of her magic mirror and demanded,

"Mirror mirror on the wall,
Who is the fairest of them all?"

And the mirror replied, "Snow White is the fairest of them all!"

When the Queen heard this, she was beside herself with jealousy and almost smashed the mirror.

But then she thought of an evil plan and sent for one of her husband's huntsmen immediately. The Queen would become the fairest of them all, once again. And the mirror would never mention Snow White, ever again.

"Ride deep into the forest," the cruel Queen commanded, "take Snow White with you and do away with her. Return to me when the deed is done!"

The poor huntsman trembled with fear, but he dared not disobey the Queen.

So he lifted Snow White onto his horse and sped out of the palace gates. How he wished with all his heart that he had not been chosen for such a terrible task.

When they reached the middle of the forest, the huntsman told Snow White what her wicked stepmother had commanded him to do.

"Please spare my life," begged Snow White with tears in her eyes. She was very frightened and didn't know what to do.

"I could never do such a dreadful thing, Snow White," said the huntsman kindly. "Run deep into the forest as quickly as you can, and never ever return to the palace!"

Then, without looking back, the huntsman left Snow White behind and galloped away.

At first Snow White felt lost and alone as she wandered through the trees... but she wasn't without friends in the dark forest.

For one by one, the creatures who lived there gathered round as if to make her feel at home.

Then some of the birds began to twitter and flutter from tree to tree.

"I do believe you want me to follow you," cried Snow White.

And sure enough, the animals began to lead her down a narrow path which opened into a clearing.

Snow White gasped. For there, bathed in sunlight, was the quaintest cottage you can imagine.

When Snow White pulled on the bell and nobody answered, she pushed open the door and stepped into the cottage.

Round a table were seven small chairs. Seven small bowls, seven small mugs and seven shiny spoons were set out neatly ready for the next meal. For this was the home of the seven dwarfs who worked hard all day long in the mountains digging for gold.

Snow White was so hungry, she helped herself to some bread and cheese and a small mug of milk.

Then she climbed the stairs and there, in a row, were seven little beds. "I'm so tired," yawned Snow White rubbing her eyes. "I'm sure whoever lives here won't mind if I rest for a while." So she pulled one of the blankets over herself and fell fast asleep.

When the seven dwarfs returned home, they realised somebody had been in their cottage. They rushed upstairs to find Snow White sleeping. "Let her rest," whispered the oldest dwarf, "for no doubt tomorrow she will tell us why she has come to our cottage."

Next morning, as soon as it was light, Snow White woke up. She tiptoed downstairs, and there waiting to greet her, were the seven dwarfs.

These little men looked so friendly and kind, Snow White was not in the least afraid as she told her story.

When they heard about the wicked Queen, the dwarfs begged her to stay as long as she wished.

But before they set off for their work, they made Snow White promise never to open the door to any stranger, for they feared that the Queen would find out where she was hiding.

Snow White had never been so happy in her life. Living with the dwarfs in their quaint little cottage made her sing and dance with joy.

She cooked and cleaned and mended their clothes, and still found plenty of time to play with the animals and birds of the forest. They watched over her all day long while the dwarfs were away, and very soon Snow White forgot all about her wicked stepmother.

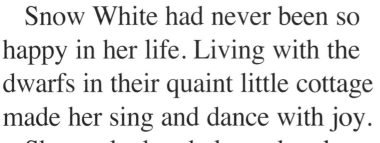

However, at the palace, the vain Queen hadn't bothered to look into her magic mirror in a long time, for she thought her huntsman had done away with Snow White in the forest.

But one day, she decided to ask the mirror,

"Mirror, mirror on the wall,
  Who is the fairest of them all?"

And the magic mirror replied, "Snow White is the fairest of them all!"

Never before had the Queen been so angry. "Where is she?" she screamed.

And the magic mirror replied,

"Beyond the mountains
There's a forest glade.
In the seven dwarfs' cottage
Lives the fairest maid!"

When she heard that, the wicked Queen quickly disguised herself as an old woman. Then, with the help of her evil charms, she made a poisonous apple which was red on one side, green on the other.

"Red and green apple shiny and bright,
The red half means death to the fair Snow White.
The green half is safe as safe can be,
And that will be eaten up by me!"

And the Queen cackled to herself as she made her way through the forest.

71

Meanwhile, Snow White waved goodbye to the seven dwarfs as they went off to work in the goldmine.

"Remember not to open the door to any strangers," they shouted as they marched off towards the mountain.

So Snow White went inside, closed the door and set about her chores.

Then to her surprise she heard a voice calling through the open window.

"Apples for sale! Buy my apples!" cried an old woman who was standing outside.

Snow White had never seen such big juicy apples and longed to taste one. However, she didn't open the cottage door.

But the wicked Queen was crafty and she cut the

apple in half.

"There's nothing to fear, my dear," she cackled as she bit into the green half.

Then she handed the poisonous red half to Snow White, who took one tiny bite and fell lifeless to the floor.

"Snow White is no more! I am still the fairest of them all!" cried the wicked Queen as she hurried back to the palace.

The moment the animals and birds heard this, they guessed what had happened and ran to warn the dwarfs.

When the seven dwarfs returned to their cottage and found their beloved Snow White, no words can describe their sorrow.

Believing her to be dead, the dwarfs made a glass casket and laid her gently inside.

Then they carried her to their favourite spot in the forest glade and watched over Snow White day and night.

The dwarfs were unsure who had done this. The oldest dwarf, who was very wise, guessed that it was the work of the wicked Queen, and he tried his best to comfort the others.

"Remember," he said, "there is no evil spell that cannot be broken."

The other dwarfs stopped crying and looked at Snow White hopefully.

One day a handsome Prince came riding through the forest. He rode on a beautiful white horse.

When he reached the glade and saw Snow White lying in her glass casket, the Prince got down from his horse and knelt down at her side. He fell in love with her at once.

And when he saw the dwarfs' unhappy faces, he begged them to tell him what had happened.

"Will you allow me to take Snow White, so she can lie in the most beautiful room in my palace?" the Prince pleaded.

The kind-hearted dwarfs knew the Prince was in love with Snow White, and she would always be safe in his care. So all seven of them agreed to let him take her.

As the Prince lifted up the glass casket, the tiny piece of poisoned apple fell from Snow White's lips.

She opened her eyes and sat up. The Prince leaned forward and gave her a kiss, and Snow White fell in love with him at that very moment. The wicked Queen's evil spell was broken at last!

The Prince asked Snow White to marry him, and she said she'd love to, and soon the wedding was arranged.

The seven dwarfs never went back to dig for gold in the mountain. They were far too busy looking after the cottage and visiting Snow White and the Prince in their palace.

As for the wicked Queen... when she looked again in her magic mirror, and she saw that Snow White was more beautiful than before... she smashed the mirror into a thousand pieces and vanished for ever in a puff of black smoke!

Favourite
Princess
Tales